About the Author

Lucrezia Scotto di Marrazzo grew up on the island of Procida, the smallest island in the Gulf of Naples. She spent her childhood learning to fish, row, and swim, but she always preferred books to outdoor activities. Although her origins are rooted in an island smaller than four kilometres, she is an explorer at heart. Her desire to travel led her to attend university abroad. She lived first in the Netherlands and then in Scotland, where she earned a Master's in Corporate Law at Edinburgh Law School. She currently lives in Luxembourg and works as a legal professional.

Caging Butterflies

Lucrezia Scotto di Marrazzo

Caging Butterflies

Olympia Publishers
London

www.olympiapublishers.com
OLYMPIA PAPERBACK EDITION

Copyright © Lucrezia Scotto di Marrazzo 2022

The right of Lucrezia Scotto di Marrazzo to be identified as author of this work has been asserted in accordance with sections 77 and 78 of the Copyright, Designs and Patents Act 1988.

All Rights Reserved

No reproduction, copy or transmission of this publication may be made without written permission.
No paragraph of this publication may be reproduced, copied or transmitted save with the written permission of the publisher, or in accordance with the provisions of the Copyright Act 1956 (as amended).

Any person who commits any unauthorised act in relation to this publication may be liable to criminal prosecution and civil claims for damage.

A CIP catalogue record for this title is available from the British Library.

ISBN: 978-1-80074-211-6

This is a work of fiction.
Names, characters, places and incidents originate from the writer's imagination. Any resemblance to actual persons, living or dead, is purely coincidental.

First Published in 2022

Olympia Publishers
Tallis House
2 Tallis Street
London
EC4Y 0AB

Printed in Great Britain

Dedication

To my parents and sister for having endured years of long car rides with my creative storytelling in the background.

And to You, for giving me the ability to produce butterflies in the dark.

All my life I have been waiting for you.

I looked for your face in strangers walking on the streets, in friendly faces, in enemies, in the mirror.

Your face was in every book I read, and in every movie I watched, where all the characters reminded me of you. Were you really there with me to watch these movies? To comment on these books?

You came to me in my dreams, sharing loving words and affectionate moments, only for us.

You made me forget everything around me. Seasons were changing, months went passing by, but I never stopped looking for you in everyone and everything.

However, I am starting to realize that maybe all this thinking was in vain. All the moments I pictured were just a product of my imagination, you were not there with me, and you are still not.

I do not know if I am ever going to find you in real life, or whether I am doomed to live looking for you in others, and then tormenting myself when my senses tell me that this man is not you.

It took just one gaze at you on a rainy November day to make me forget the line between imagination and reality. What is real? What is not? Are you here? Am I alone?

All my life I have been waiting for you and I will not let you go easily. I will still look for you in every bystander, in every picture and every perfume.

But I am growing up and I need to go on with my life; I need you to set me free. To leave me alone, so that I can meet someone else, who looks like you, but whom I can touch, I can kiss, and I can laugh with. Can you do that for me, my imaginary love?

Not Loving

People say that to love is to live in pain.
 But to never love is even more painful. How many imaginary kisses can I share with the object of my love, knowing that they will never be real? How many words will remain unspoken? How many butterflies can a human produce in his stomach, knowing that they will remain caged and unable to fly?

Fools

Not loving is hard, impossible really; When people say "The heart wants what it wants", they are right because there is nothing we can do when faced with the internal movements of our heart. Fools: that is what we are; just a tremendous group of fools. How long can we pretend that we don't love? That we don't feel that our heart is going to explode at the mere sight of the object of our love? How long can we lie to ourselves and pretend that we have our feelings under control? Fools.
 Everything is already happening inside of us and we have yet to discover the power of our own emotions. And when we do find it, we will blame every inch of our bodies for not having listened to ourselves. Fools.

The encounter

The first time I saw you, it was a warm day in late June.

Our eyes encountered each other for a few seconds, but that was enough to ignite the engine of my imagination.

You were shy, sitting in the chair by yourself; while I conversed with others, not paying much attention to their words, because I was focusing on your beautiful eyes on me.

I felt them looking at me, at my hair, my body and my soul.

I wanted to come to you and introduce myself. I wanted to walk in your direction and look into your eyes. I wanted to come close to you, without saying anything, because my eyes would express it all.

But I couldn't; my feet wouldn't move. And not because I was afraid, but because I had already given my heart to someone else and I couldn't take it away.

So, I ran in the opposite direction and left, only to return months later.

That day, I never turned back to you, to see if you were looking at me. I didn't have to. I knew you were.

At that time, no butterfly sparked yet within me.

You

You don't know what it means to be noticed by you. And not because I can't have the attention of others, but because you pull strings in my heart that I didn't know I had.

Months will go by, years will pass, but I already know you will forever be the one who saved me at the time I needed to see light the most.

Playing, playing

It was just supposed to be a game, a bet between friends. The first one of us you would have spoken to would be declared the winner. And when I won, the game should have stopped there. But I didn't want to stop. I didn't want it to stop, that incredible sensation of feeling alive after a long time in the darkness. And so, I told myself that it would be more amusing to prolong the game, to see where it would lead me. But this time, I was the only one playing; playing with my feelings and giving the butterflies free entrance into my body.

And where did it lead me? To a different reality where speaking to you once a day, was no longer enough. I had to discover everything about you, to find ways to see you more often. I knew I had to run away, to put a stop to the game. But the feelings were too strong; so strong that I would think to myself "one more day, just one more day of playing". And when that day came, reality was just not an option to return to. Was I weak? Was I foolish? I don't know. But I was desperately looking for a way to escape the first reality, that I had to create a second one, where your eyes and my imagination could shape a better world to live in. And so, the predator became the prey, the strong became the weak; playing became living and imagination became reality.

The elevator

I tried to forget you. To forget about those beautiful eyes, that caged me and held me prisoner for the entire summer.

But just like a magnet, you attracted me to your soul and mine was fully electrified.

I tried to imagine what our next encounter would be like and if you would recognize me, or if I was just a lone star that didn't shine in your universe.

Then fate gave me another signal. And, I met you, of all people, in front of the elevator.

My heart sank and I didn't even dare to look into your eyes, afraid of getting lost in them.

We entered the elevator and I could see your eyes attracting mine, two souls wanting to explore one another.

"Which floor?" you asked me.

"All the way up" I replied.

Illness

The butterflies are starting to develop in my stomach.

I feel them growing and taking power. They fly in every direction, and all have different colours.

There is no harmony in their movement, they do not move close to one another; instead, they fly wherever they like, and wherever they need to. They behave like a confused group that wanders around after losing its leader.

They begin to spread and, from the stomach, invade all parts of my body. They are infecting my organs, my bloodstream and my heart.

They make my legs soft and shaky, to the point that I am unable to move.

My pupils dilate, my heart keeps racing at the sight of him, and I have goosebumps all over my arms and legs.

And the worst part is, there is nothing I can do about it. I can't stop them.

Now, they are in control.

Your eyes

Oh, the way you make me feel even with a simple gaze. And after all this time, it's still that awkward looking into each other's eyes and then slowly pulling away, that flames my spirit.

We need mystery, we need hope, and we need a pair of eyes to look deep into our souls when we lose the ability to do so ourselves.

We run into so many faces every day,

but catching the attention of a pair of eyes is what feeds our hearts.

I will always remember the first time our eyes met. Yes, because even before I knew your name, even before I knew the power you had over me, my eyes already knew in which direction to look. And so, they sent a signal to the heart and put it in motion, after it had been rusty for so long. And then they sent a signal to my brain, that registered your image, making sure it would remain inside me forever.

Killing butterflies

I have been trying to suppress these feelings, these butterflies that invaded my body and flow in my blood.

I want to kill them, stop them, because they are the cause of all this confusion.

If only there was a way to cage them for good and throw away the key.

But the cage is imaginary, and the butterflies are escaping.

They fly, then multiply and continue spreading.

They want to give me a signal of their presence.

They want to taunt me, because I am just a weak human who believes she can cage butterflies.

Involuntary muscle

"What is the human heart? It is a muscular organ that beats and contracts without our control".

How does Love define the heart?

"A centre of energy that beats in synchronization with the emotions of its owner, without depending on him or his commands to function".

The heart already knows how to function. Do not try to change it or force it into another course.

It will always find its way back.

Dreaming

Sometimes I wonder whether I crave a relationship with you,
 or whether I crave the thought of having a relationship with you.
 Am I in love with you or with the dream of you?
 Am I in love with your features or with the thought of having you in my arms?

Opening doors

And ever since you started wandering in my mind,
 I have never locked the door or forbidden you to enter.
 Because even if I wished to close the front door,
 You will always have the keys to the back one.

Crossing the line

You are the line I need to cross to move from reality to imagination.

The art exhibit

I am trying, trying to move on with my life. I am trying to forget you.
 But the butterflies are always there; a constant reminder of my true feelings and the chances I am not taking, the happiness I am not allowing myself to feel, and the time I am wasting.

And before I know it, I find myself looking at you, sitting next to you, and appreciating music I have never heard, just because you like it.

My brain says "Enough! This is all nonsense. You are an adult, a rational being. Take control of your emotions". I want to do that, to scream and show my brain that I can control my emotions. But I find myself helpless, captured inside the thought of you; The way you smile at me among so many faces, is a painting permanently exposed in the art exhibit that the butterflies are setting up for me.

But I still refuse to look at it.

Fighting

I am not sure what I feel for you. But whatever this is,
    it makes me feel alive. More than ever.

But it also makes me feel trapped; because the longer I am apart from the real you, the longer I am caged in this nightmare, where you are just a part of my imagination.

And where I have to fight with myself between making you real or continue to feast on imaginary thoughts.

I am coming for you

And for every step we take to reach one another, there is a rope that pulls us back to the start. Are we doomed for eternity to never touch each other's hands or is the universe pulling us apart only to strengthen our path?

Your name

Oh, the chills your name gives me. Those few letters have now acquired a new, precious meaning because they evoke your figure in my brain, which in turn makes my heart jump and brightens my day. Every little thing reminds me of you, and I couldn't go back to a world where the echo of your name didn't give me those chills. Because after all this time, these words are the only things that bind my soul to yours.
The anchor I need to escape reality and cuddle into imagination.

To kill a butterfly

The turning point has arrived. I have taken a decision.
　　I cannot live this way any more, I cannot pretend any longer, and I cannot let these insects control me.
　　'*To Kill a Butterfly*' is a manual that no one ever thought necessary to write.
　　But how can I hurt something inside of me, without hurting myself?
　　I begin to make a list of possible solutions. Poison, cutting, punching, and screaming are not helpful.
　　I can hear the butterflies mocking me, saying that I can try anything I want to get rid of them, but they will never go away.
　　I am only human; what can I do against them if I cannot even control my own emotions?
　　And then I think about it. I have an idea.
　　I could actually put them in a cage. I must build a

cage and restrict their movement. Soon they will not be able to fly any more or multiply. Soon they will not interfere with other parts of my body.

What is reality?

And if we all live in a dream, then reality is just our personal nightmare.

It is confrontation with reality that scares me the most.

What if you didn't like me? What if you didn't fall for me? What if you have no butterflies within you? These questions don't scare me. I can live with them.

But please don't take away the magic that my brain develops when I think of you, when I think of us together, and when I feel my body trembling and my heart stumbling at the mere thought, that you may be near.

If everything is just enclosed in my mind and reality is a mixture of memories and imagination, then I should be the one in charge of these thoughts.

That's why I keep on dreaming, waiting for the day when the dream turns into truth, and you are here, present in the moment, with me.

And if that doesn't happen, I will continue to wait and lure my brain towards self- made emotions.

Because in the end, our brain does not understand the difference between reality and imagination. Instead, it recognizes the emotions we feel, whether they are real or a product of our dreaming.

And, fuelled by emotions, the brain stimulates the heart that pumps the blood and uplifts the organs. And all of this makes us feel alive.

No guilt

Why is it that every time I allow myself to think of you, the butterflies of love take advantage over the worms of guilt?

The metal cage

So, I start building a metal cage in my stomach. I attract the butterflies with honey, and as I imagined, it works.

They all gather in the cage, and I can almost hear their wings moving faster and faster as they try to break free, and then stopping when they realise they cannot do anything any more. They are trapped.

The cage is locked.

And so, for some months, I do not see him any more and, like the butterflies, I cage my feelings too, as I try to commence a new chapter in my life.

All is dark

Months go by, and I try to forget about you. And, with the butterflies in the cage, it seems to work.

I go back to my routine, my traditional life.

But soon I realise that none of the things I did before is still the same.

My appetite has vanished; I refuse to go outside, and I often find myself with my head in the clouds, whistling a melody whose words I do not know.

I bury myself in books, finding comfort in the complex relationships of imaginary characters.

But everything around me is dark. Everything is grey, dull, rainy, and cold. As my heart becomes sad, so does my appearance.

I feel numb, and as the days go by, this reality turns into a nightmare.

I turn into a ghost, with no expression, no life, and no love.

Before

As the new year commences, I find myself returning to the place that gave me happiness at a time when I felt lifeless.

For indeed, before my eyes met his, I was an anonymous person.

I would wake up, eat, walk, drink, sleep and repeat.

But everything I used to do before seemed pointless now.

Books no longer made me feel alive. No landscape was as beautiful when I didn't have the right person to admire it with.

No food is as tasty, and no water brings refreshment when you turn into a lifeless object, wearing the same clothes and waiting for the end of each uneventful day.

Minutes

Because for every minute I spend trying to move on with my life,

There are five minutes I spend thinking of you.

Pieces

But, just like every dreamer, the time came for me to face the cruel reality, which is always present and ready to show us that we should not take refuge in dreams to escape from a truth that we are too afraid to face.

Reality arrived for me on a cold day in late March, shattering my imagination into pieces that I am still trying to pick up. I saw you entering the room with someone else, hand in hand, heart to heart.

You walked past me without even noticing I was standing there, too focused on new eyes to look into my old soul.

And just like that, I became a ghost again, shapeless, without form, without feelings. Someone who no longer radiated light, someone not worthy of your attention. It was at that moment that reality cut me deeply like a thousand knives and forced me to open my eyes to a living condition from which I had tried with all my might to free myself.

What scared me the most was not seeing you with someone else but rather losing that privileged place in your life, or at least the place I thought you had reserved for me. Your attention was the cord that had been attaching me to a happier, finer and warmer reality, filled with dreams, butterflies and strong feelings. But now that your attention had shifted onto someone else, I felt myself falling back into the dark hole, where imagination was not envisioned and where butterflies were not able to fly, and boredom prevailed over everything else. I tried to scream, to call your name as I fell, but you could not hear me.

Then again, why would you turn your attention to yet another ghost?

They fly again

When the moment comes, and I see him again, I fight the urge to move in his direction.

And then I hear it, a dull noise from within that makes my stomach hurt again.

And my legs are shaking, my hands are numb, and my face turns pale at the sight of him. I run away. I am too scared.

A severe fever develops inside me, and this time it is harder to fight it.

And then I feel them again, those butterflies, flying back into my stomach and expanding through my vital organs.

But that is not possible, I have caged them.

I must be hallucinating. I must be going mad to even perceive, that insects could grow inside me.

I am the one feeling trapped now. How can few tiny insects outweigh my willpower? I feel lost and scared, and before I know it, I am on my knees with my hands covering my face.

I am tired, so tired of feeling this way, and I am mad at myself for being unable to find happiness in what I already have. Because I can't; not any more. Not since I discovered that there is another human being, able to bring so much more light, into my darkness.

The sight of him is warmth for my feelings, for my body and my soul. But it is a disease for my brain, that cannot accept this situation.

As I predicted, the butterflies found their way out of the cage. They are free and happy to torment me again.

Alone in my sadness, I begin to cry.

They seem to take this action as a sign of weakness; they begin to fly around me, taunting me, confusing me more.

I scream at them, tell them to stop, that I cannot do this any more. I had my life, and now I am losing control of it.

But they do not stop. Instead, they fly faster, and the movement of their wings, so imprecise and disharmonious, is painful.

I have weakened again and I return to crying on the floor.

But then one of them stops and starts talking to me.

She takes pity on me and on my human weakness. "Stop crying", she says; "There is no reason to. Something beautiful is happening inside of you'.

"How can this be something beautiful? I say, pointing to my body. "My actions are out of my control. My hands tremble, my legs don't move, my heart begins to race for no reason, and my mouth goes dry.'

She laughs. "What you have just described is what we live for; honey may attract ordinary butterflies, but it is love that fuels us."

"Then why don't you leave me and go to

live inside someone else?"

'Because we don't choose the person to live in; it is the human who produces us, who creates us and gives purpose to our lives. In this moment, you have an incredible power stemming from your heart. You are giving life; you are generating it. What you feel for this person is something that many people experience in the course of their lives, but that not everyone is brave enough to embrace".

It is called Love and if you don't let it pass by, it will be the greatest, most beautiful and wonderful sensation you will get to experience in all your years.

Don't be afraid. Accept your feelings, and you will be free. Fail to do so, and you will be a slave to your own emotions.'

I yell back; "I don't want you here. You are just creating problems for me. Please tell me how to get you out of my body".

She smiles again.

"You can't take us away; you can't move us. We are here because you want us to be here. To make you feel what you are feeling now, to give you the courage to accept your feelings. And if you do, we will stay here for a long time. And the pain will turn into happiness, and you will learn to love us because we are signs of emotions you didn't know you could produce.

Let us stay here and show you the way. Don't be afraid; it is natural, beautiful, and above all, impossible to control.

You don't have to do anything; just let us touch the cords of your heart and make you feel alive".

Thank you

I don't know if you are aware of it, but in just a few months, you impacted my life more than many people did in years. Now that reality is becoming a mixture of fading memories and imagination, all I want to say to you is 'thank you'.

Thank you because you gave me back the excitement of living another day with you in it.

Thank you because you make my heart sink, my mind wander, and my eyes smile. And thank you because those feelings make me less abstract and more human. Thank you because when I see you, I know it is going to be a good day.

Thank you because you made me escape reality for a while and taught me what it feels like to dream again.

Thank you; because you came so abruptly into my life and allowed me to see the light again.

Thank you; because you gave me something I had been craving for a long time without knowing it: attention.

And thank you, because through you,

I found the way back to myself.

www.ingramcontent.com/pod-product-compliance
Lightning Source LLC
LaVergne TN
LVHW041554060526
838200LV00037B/1280